This Little Tiger book belongs to:

_____

_____

_____

For Michael, with all my love – C F
For Emily – S M

LITTLE TIGER PRESS LTD,
an imprint of the Little Tiger Group,
1 Coda Studios, 189 Munster Road, London SW6 6AW
www.littletiger.co.uk

First published in Great Britain 2009
This edition published 2017

Text copyright © Claire Freedman 2009
Illustrations copyright © Simon Mendez 2009
Claire Freedman and Simon Mendez have asserted their rights
to be identified as the author and illustrator of this work under
the Copyright, Designs and Patents Act, 1988

A CIP catalogue record for this book is available
from the British Library

Printed in China • LTP/1800/2847/0719

2 4 6 8 10 9 7 5 3

One Winter's Night

Claire Freedman   Simon Mendez

LiTTLE TiGER

LONDON

It was deepest, darkest winter. Wild snow
blizzards had howled through the woods
for days and the animals had been hiding
in their dens, cold and hungry.

But tonight, suddenly, all was quiet and
the sky was clear.

Fox peeped from his snowy den. Out of
the darkness appeared a lone figure,
a badger, gleaming silver in the moonlight.

"Hello," Badger called gently.
"Please, I'm so hungry. Do you
have any food to share?"

Fox frowned. He had hardly
enough food for himself. But
there was such a kind look in
Badger's eyes. Fox felt he *had*
to help him.

"Wait here," he said.

"Thank you," Badger smiled, gratefully taking the few berries Fox offered. Then off Badger went into the snow, head bent against the bitter wind.

Mouse was much too cold and hungry to sleep.
As she tossed and turned in her bed, suddenly
she heard footsteps outside. "My, oh my!"
she gasped. "Who's out at this time of night?"

"Hello!" a silvery figure called softly.
"Please, I'm very hungry. Do you have
any spare food?"

"I've nothing at all!" Mouse grumbled.
"There's no food anywhere!"

"I understand," Badger nodded,
and he turned to go.

Mouse listened as the heavy crunch of Badger's footsteps slowly faded. Badger had seemed so gentle and caring. Yet she had turned him away.

"Wait!" Mouse scampered after him. "Hare lives nearby. Maybe she can help!"

Together, Mouse and Badger struggled to Hare's house. The wind whipped. Snowflakes swirled. But somehow, even in the shadowy dark, Mouse felt safe beside Badger, his warm eyes twinkling like bright stars.

Hare was rather cross to be woken up.
And she didn't really want to share the small
handful of berries she'd saved with *anyone*!

"I know it's late, Hare, but I told Badger
you might help," Mouse whispered. "He's
freezing cold and starving. And so am I!"

"I suppose you had both better come in
then," said Hare.

Mouse, Hare and Badger nibbled
on Hare's last few berries.

   Hare thought back to when
times were much kinder.
Then, she and Mouse had
spent happy days together,
sharing everything. Hare
missed those times.

All too soon, Badger thanked them and left. Without him the burrow felt colder, and the night darker.

"Poor Badger – it's freezing outside!"
Mouse sighed, peering out into the
frosty darkness.
      "I hope he'll be all right,"
Hare said anxiously.
      Just then they spotted a shadowy
figure moving slowly towards them . . .

"It's Fox!" cried Mouse.

"What are *you* doing here?"
Hare asked him.

"I'm searching for Badger!"
Fox explained. "He was so
exhausted and hungry!"

Mouse and Hare nodded.
They were worried about
Badger too.

"I think we should go out
and look for him," Mouse said.

In the shimmering snow, Badger's footprints were pools of silver.

The blizzard blew stronger still as the three friends followed Badger's silvery tracks deeper and deeper into the woods.

"Over there!" pointed Fox at last.

There was Badger asleep amongst the roots
of a tree, covered in a frosting of snow.
"He's frozen!" gasped Mouse. "Poor Badger!"
"We must help him," Fox cried.

Quietly, so as not to wake
him, Mouse and Hare
gathered some soft mosses
and leaves for Badger's bed.
Fox dug a snowy shelter to
keep him snug.

Then together they curled up cosy
and warm in their snowy den.
The wind howled and snow fell
thickly, but they had never
slept so well.

The next morning Badger had gone!
The friends looked around and saw
a trail of silvery footprints stretching
far into the distance.

"I wonder where Badger is going now?" said Fox, "and if he'll ever visit us again?"

But just then, Mouse gave an excited shout. "Look! Over there!"

Everyone stared in surprise.

"What a wonderful gift!" Fox gasped.

"It's magic!" Mouse whispered. Then she spotted the tiny message:

In every caring thing you do,
The love you give comes back to you!

"It's from Badger!" Hare cried. "We all *knew* he was special!"

The sun suddenly burst through and a million snowflakes sparkled – bright as the twinkle in Badger's smiling eyes!